CHARLIE
and the New Baby

To all the big brothers and big sisters of the world
—Ree

When cooking, it is important to keep safety in mind. Children should always ask
permission from an adult before cooking and should be supervised by an adult in the
kitchen at all times. The publisher and author disclaim any liability from any injury that
might result from the use, proper or improper, of the recipe contained in this book.

CHARLIE
and the New Baby

by Ree Drummond

illustrations by Diane deGroat

HARPER

An Imprint of HarperCollinsPublishers

Well, howdy!

Charlie the Ranch Dog here. You can just
call me Charlie.

Life sure is good out here on the ol' ranch.
The sun is shining, the kids are playing, the
birds are chirping, the cattle are happy . . .

. . . And Mama is rubbing my belly. I love it when Mama rubs my belly.

Ahhh . . . . Life doesn't get any better than this. It's good to be the King of the Ranch!

Snort—HUH?
What'd I miss?

Where are the kids?
Where's Mama?

Wait,
what's that?

They're carrying a **CALF!**

What's going on?
What are they DOING?

Wait . . .
they're taking the calf . . .
IN THE HOUSE?!?

But everyone KNOWS calves don't belong in the house!

I'd better go investigate.

I have now officially seen everything.

Well, this calf DOES look brand-new. She must be a brand-new baby.

Maybe she's lonely. Maybe she has lost her mama. Maybe she needs a little tender loving care.

Mama and the kids are perfect for that job! They give me tender loving care all the time!

They scratch my ears. . . .

They feed me lunch. . . .

(Lunch is my life.)

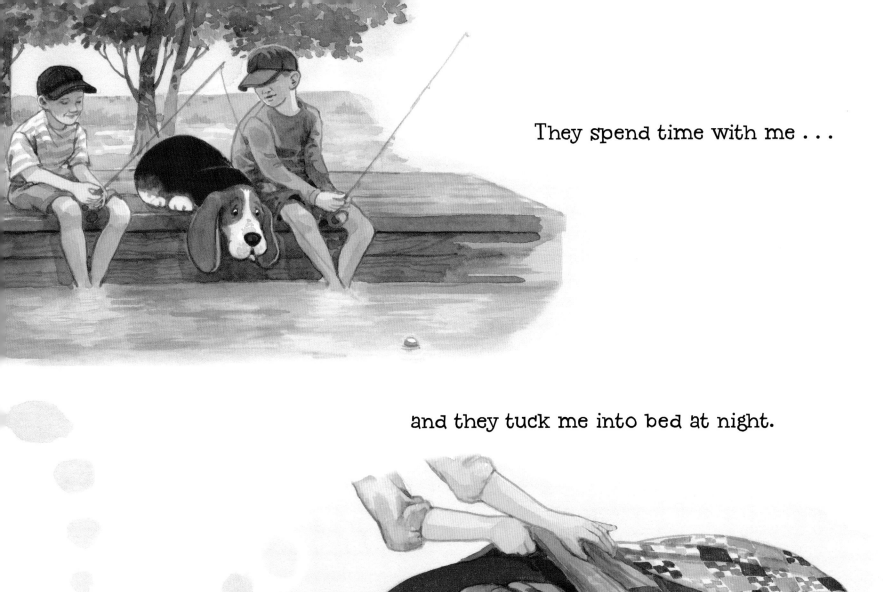

They spend time with me . . .

and they tuck me into bed at night.

Yep, it's all TLC, all the time for me. . . .

Hey! That's my blanket!

I've always loved that blanket.

Now they're giving the calf . . . **a bath?**

Hmm. It's been awhile since I've had one of those.

Wait, where's Mama going?
Maybe she's making me dinner!

Yum.
Dinner is my life.

Wait.

What?

HUH?!?

Hark. Do you hear that sound?
That's the sound of my stomach growling.
I haven't eaten in a long, long time.
At least an hour!
I'm so hungry, I could faint.

Hey! Now they're tucking her in. In MY bed!
That's exactly how they tuck ME in!

Boy, that soft bed of mine sure does look comfy.

Is it bedtime already?
But what about my bed?
What?
I have to sleep on the floor?
Oh, no. Say it ain't so.

Oh, well. Nothing really left to do but get some shut-eye, I guess.

Maybe I'll dream about a happier time long, long ago.

A time when a dog could lie on his own bed.

A time when a dog could get a bath and a belly rub from time to time.

A time before this silly ol' calf ever showed up.

A time when . . .

When . . .

ZZZZZZZZZZZ . . .

Snort—HUH?!?

Uh-oh.

Ahh. Now this is more like it!

Don't worry, everyone. There's plenty of me to go around.

And looks like there's enough tender loving care around here for everyone. EVEN ABIGAIL!

Charlie's Favorite Egg-in-a-Hole

Makes one serving

Be safe! Always cook with an adult.
Don't touch sharp knives or hot stoves
and ovens! And always wash your hands
before and after cooking.

Ingredients

1 slice of your favorite kind of bread
1 tablespoon butter
1 whole egg
Salt to taste
Pepper to taste

Instructions

1. With a biscuit cutter or the rim of a glass, press a hole in the center of the slice of bread.

2. Next, heat a skillet over medium-low heat and melt a tablespoon of butter in it. When the butter is all spread out, place the piece of bread in the skillet and crack the egg straight into the center of the hole.

3. Cook for at least 30 seconds or so before attempting to move the bread or things could get messy. Sprinkle the egg with salt and pepper to taste. After about a minute, flip it all over with a spatula and salt and pepper the other side.

4. Now move the whole piece of toast around the skillet, soaking up all the glorious butter. Let it cook until the yolk feels soft without feeling overly jiggly.